Winter Waits

By Lynn Plourde

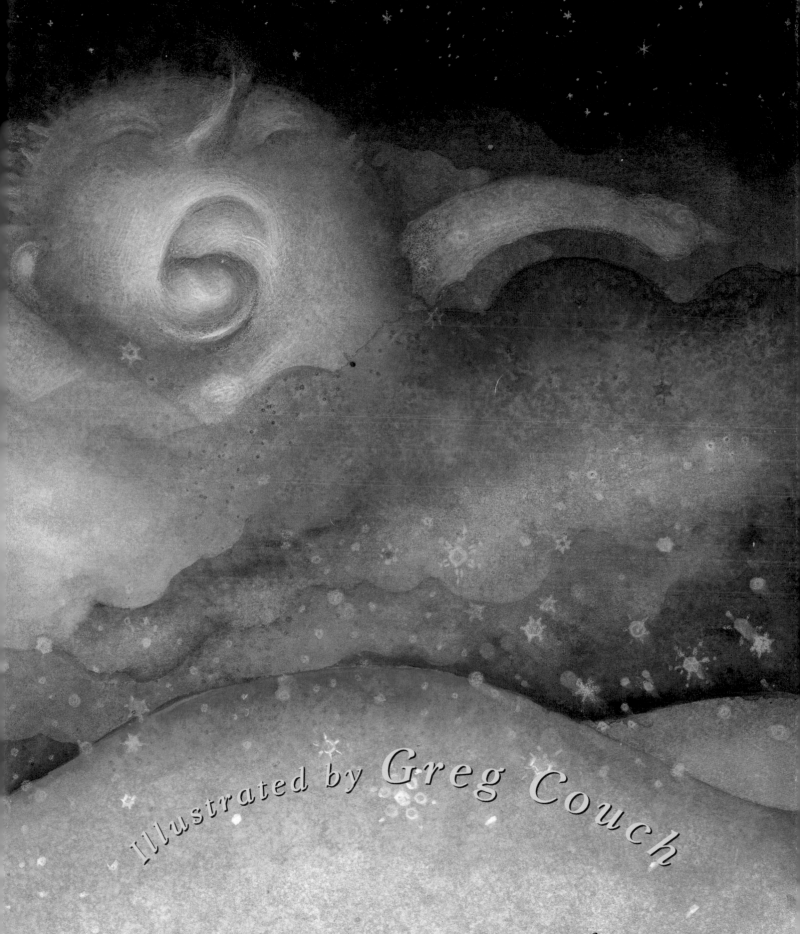

Illustrated by Greg Couch

Simon & Schuster Books for Young Readers

New York   London   Toronto   Sydney   Singapore

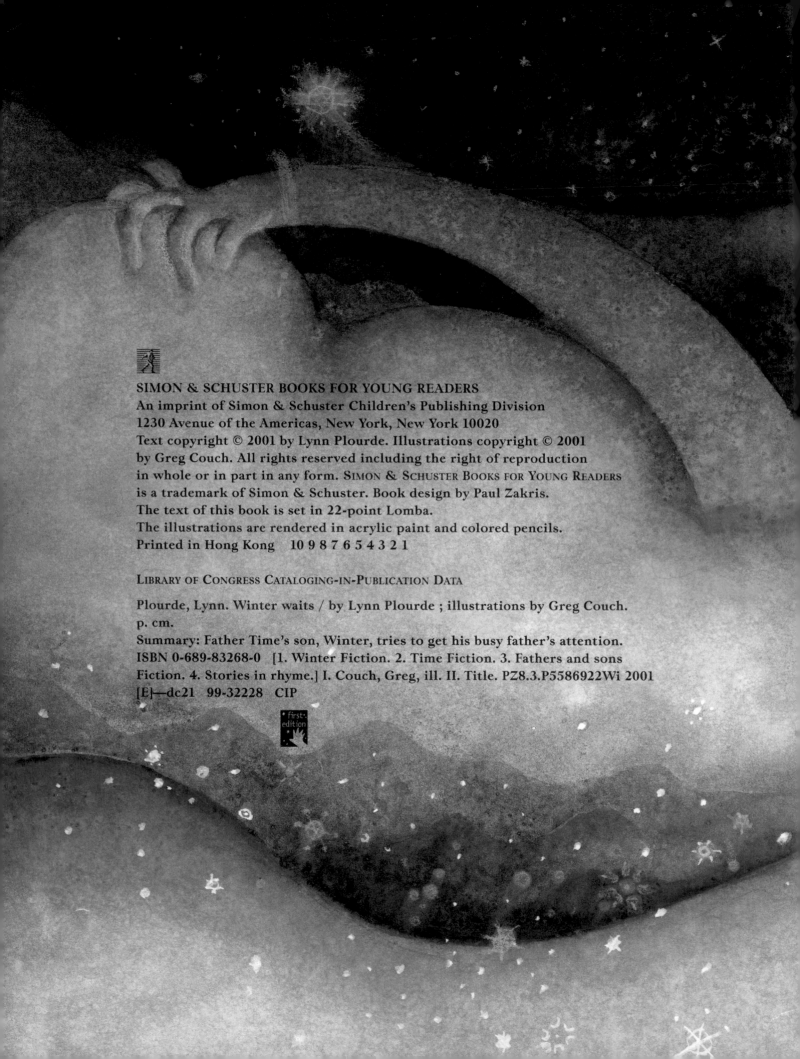

SIMON & SCHUSTER BOOKS FOR YOUNG READERS

An imprint of Simon & Schuster Children's Publishing Division

1230 Avenue of the Americas, New York, New York 10020

Text copyright © 2001 by Lynn Plourde. Illustrations copyright © 2001
by Greg Couch. All rights reserved including the right of reproduction
in whole or in part in any form. SIMON & SCHUSTER BOOKS FOR YOUNG READERS
is a trademark of Simon & Schuster. Book design by Paul Zakris.
The text of this book is set in 22-point Lomba.
The illustrations are rendered in acrylic paint and colored pencils.
Printed in Hong Kong   10 9 8 7 6 5 4 3 2 1

LIBRARY OF CONGRESS CATALOGING-IN-PUBLICATION DATA

Plourde, Lynn. Winter waits / by Lynn Plourde ; illustrations by Greg Couch.
p. cm.
Summary: Father Time's son, Winter, tries to get his busy father's attention.
ISBN 0-689-83268-0 [1. Winter Fiction. 2. Time Fiction. 3. Fathers and sons
Fiction. 4. Stories in rhyme.] I. Couch, Greg, ill. II. Title. PZ8.3.P5586922Wi 2001
[E]—dc21 99-32228 CIP

To Dad with love—thanks for taking the time
—L. P.

For Lynn—whose words always inspire me
—G. C.

Mother Earth spies Winter
bouncing on the bed.
"Go see Father," she says,
patting his head.

So Winter sprints
across the way.
"Father, Father,
come on, let's play."

Father Time smiles
and kisses his son.
"Not now, I must work,
my littlest one."

So Winter waits
for an hour or two,
painting the grass
with a frosty hue.

He whistens and glistens
the world in white
till it spangles and sparkles
ever so bright.

"Father, Father,
come see what I did.
I painted a picture
bigger than big."

Father Time turns
and picks up his son.
"Just a minute, big guy.
My work's not done."

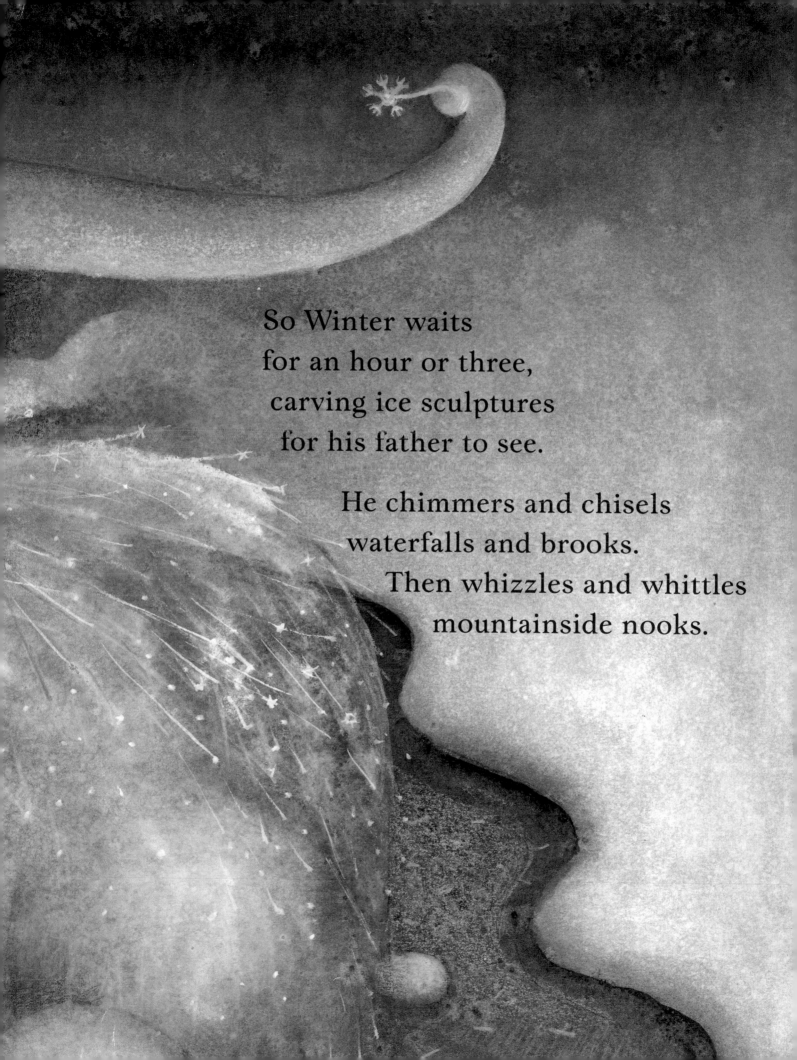

So Winter waits
for an hour or three,
carving ice sculptures
for his father to see.

He chimmers and chisels
waterfalls and brooks.
Then whizzles and whittles
mountainside nooks.

"Father, Father,
come see what I made.
A giant ice statue
where water once sprayed."

Father Time pauses
to muss his son's hair.
"When I finish my work,
I'll be right there."

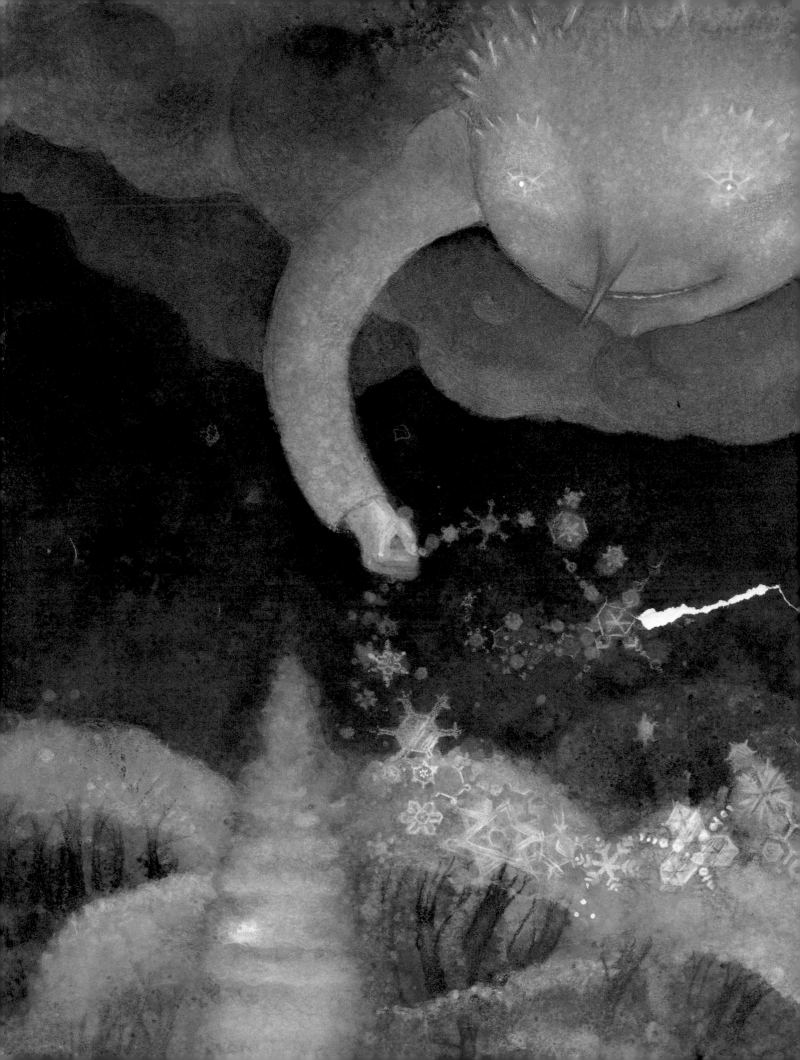

So Winter waits
for an hour or four,
cutting out snowflakes.
A few, then more.

He snizzes and snips
lacy designs.
Sprools and sprinkles them
on meadows and pines.

"Father, Father,
here's a present for you.
I made it myself.
I hope it will do."

Father Time bends,
a tear in his eye.
"Thank you, my son.
You fill me with pride."

Then Father Time tosses
his son way up high.
"Enough work for now.
Let's play in the sky."

Father and son
spring from the ground
and shake out a blizzard
that swirls all around.

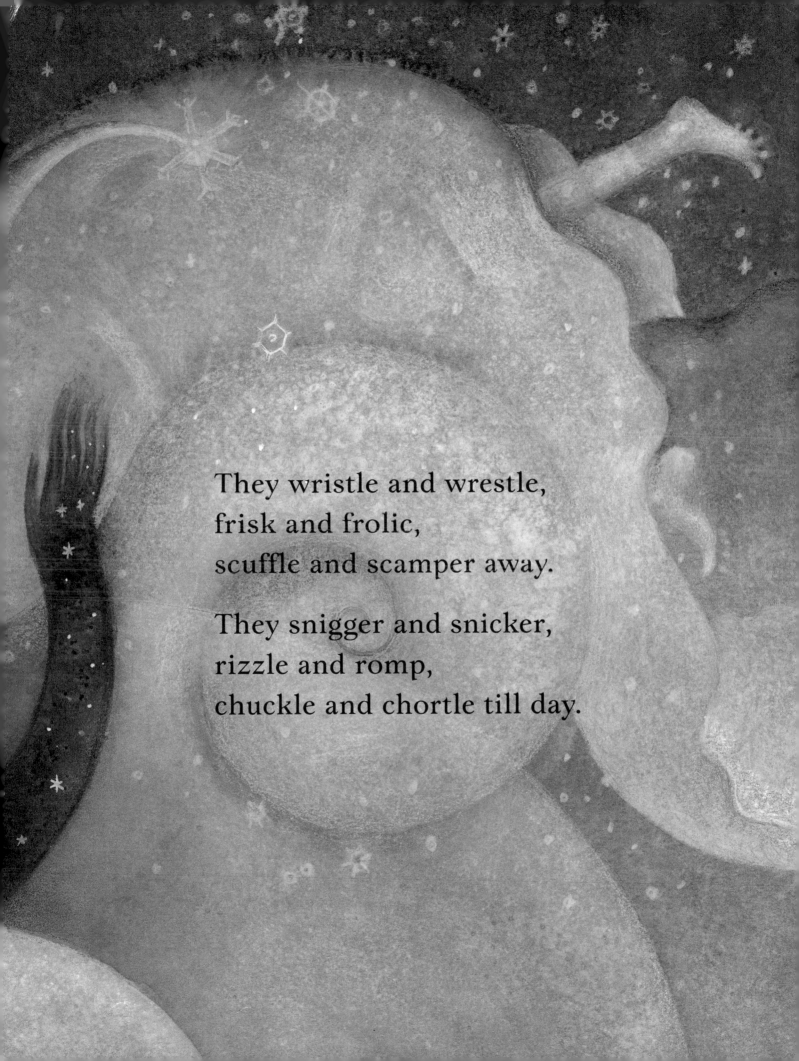

They wristle and wrestle,
frisk and frolic,
scuffle and scamper away.

They snigger and snicker,
rizzle and romp,
chuckle and chortle till day.

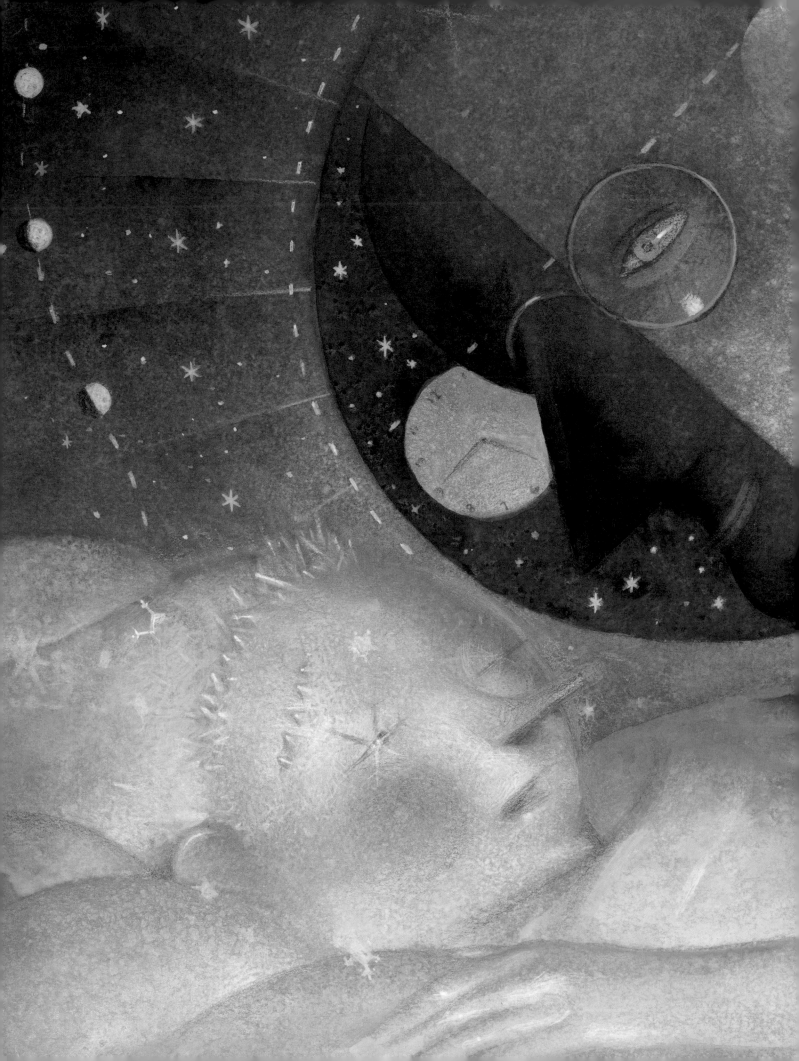

At last, so drowsy,
cuddled in a drift,
Winter starts to doze
after a sleep-tight kiss.

But he opens one eye,
asks a question then.
"Father, do you
have to work again?"

"I should set the clocks
to start the New Year.
But so what if I'm late?
I'd rather be here."

Son and father,
father and son,
snuggle up close,
till their dreams become one.

SSSSHHHHH!
Mother Earth tiptoes,
barely making a peep.
She must make sure
Spring doesn't oversleep.